the apple tree

Lynley Dodd

GARETH STEVENS

Grandpa gave Beth and Michael
an apple tree.
They planted it next to the wall,
watered it
and waited.

All winter,
the wind howled, the snow fell
and the rain lashed.
The apple tree stayed the same,
bare and still.
Beth and Michael waited.

Spring came.
One morning, there were green shoots
on the apple tree.

The green shoots turned into leaves,
shiny and new.

Then there were blossoms,
pink and white.
Bees buzzed busily
all over the tree.
Beth and Michael waited.

The blossoms withered
and blew away.

In their place, there were fat bumps
on the stalks
which grew
and grew . . .

. . . and grew into apples
the size of marbles,
then the size of ping pong balls,
then the size of tennis balls.
Beth and Michael still waited.

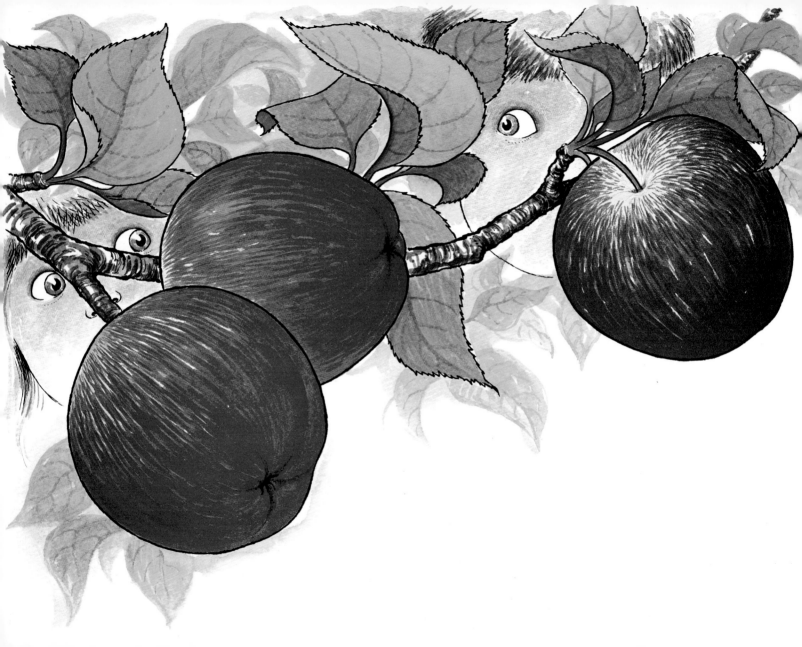

At last the apples were ready,
big and round and red.
"We'll pick them tomorrow,"
said Beth and Michael.

But that night,
a hungry possum sneaked up
and . . .

SCRUNCH! CRACKLE! SHLURP!

he ate the whole lot,
stalks, seeds and all.

THE END

Acknowledgement

This book was written with the assistance of the Choysa Bursary,
funded jointly by Quality Packers Ltd. and the New Zealand Literary Fund.
The author gratefully acknowledges their support.

Publication has been assisted by a grant from the Children's Publication Fund.

ISBN 0-918831-08-3 lib. bdg.
ISBN 0-918831-28-8 trade bdg.

North American edition first published in 1985 by
Gareth Stevens, Inc.
2408 North Farwell Avenue
Milwaukee, Wisconsin 53211

First published by
Mallinson Rendel Publishers Ltd.

Typography by Sharon Burris.